BE VERY MUCH
AFRAID

by Anne Schraff

Perfection Learning® Corporation
Logan, Iowa 51546

Cover Design: Mark Hagenberg

Cover Image Credit: © Gene Blevins/LA Daily
News/Corbis

For information, contact:
Perfection Learning® Corporation
1000 North Second Avenue, P.O. Box 500,
Logan, Iowa 51546-0500.
Phone: 1-800-831-4190 • Fax: 1-800-543-2745
perfectionlearning.com

PB ISBN-13: 978-0-7891-6572-5 ISBN-10: 0-7891-6572-4
RLB ISBN-13: 978-0-7569-4600-5 ISBN-10: 0-7569-4600-x

4 5 6 7 8 9 PP 12 11 10 09 08 07

1 "KERRY," HER MOM CALLED from downstairs, "you're doing your homework, aren't you?"

Kerry Hoffman sat at the computer and rolled her eyes. She had to do a report on Frederick Douglass for history and was researching on the Internet. Kerry was a good student, but her mom still checked on her all the time.

"Mom," Kerry yelled, "I'm a sophomore in high school! You don't have to remind me to do my homework every single day. I *know* I need to do it, okay?"

"Well," her mom called back, "how do I know you're not playing some silly game on the computer or checking out music? I just want you to do well in school, babe, that's all."

Kerry glared at the computer screen. Sometimes she felt like skipping her homework assignments and just slipping to a C in all her classes. She was so tired of her mom keeping track of every detail of her life. Kerry's mom called it responsible parenting, but sometimes Kerry felt like she was on detention 24 hours a day.

Kerry turned off the computer and called her friend, Vanessa Bassett. "Van, I could just scream! Mom keeps me on such a tight leash. I mean, she watches every move I make! She still thinks I'm a dumb little kid who needs to have her nose wiped!"

"My mom gets on my case sometimes too," Vanessa said.

"Not like *my* mother!" Kerry said bitterly. "Oh, gotta go; Grampy's coming." Kerry quickly hung up the phone. Her grandfather, whom she called Grampy, was making his way down the hallway. He had suffered a mild stroke last year, so her mom had insisted he come live with the family. Kerry's grandfather used to be a photographer who specialized in human interest and travel work.

"I'm going for a walk, Julie," Grampy called down to his daughter, Kerry's mom.

"Oh, Dad," Kerry's mom said, "it's kind of chilly outside. Are you sure that's a wise idea? You don't want to catch a cold."

"I need a walk," he said in a determined voice.

Kerry rolled her eyes again. She treats him like she treats me, she thought. We're in the same boat, Grampy and me. Her mom was one of the most controlling people Kerry had ever met. Her grandfather was 78 years old, but her mom still treated him like a child.

"Dad, there's a kind of mist coming down. I'm afraid it'll start to rain, and you'll get wet and . . ." her mom continued scolding as Kerry's grandfather came down the stairs.

"I survived monsoons in India and hurricanes in Florida, Julie. I'm going for a walk now," Kerry's grandfather said. The door closed after him.

"He is so stubborn," Kerry's mom complained to her dad. "And I've noticed he's been acting strangely lately, Peter. I think he's a little bit senile. I worry about him roaming around the streets like this . . ."

"Grampy's not senile," Kerry said to herself. "He's smart and sharp. He's the only adult in this family who treats me with a little dignity!"

Kerry went to the window and watched her grandfather marching down the street. He loved to walk. He always took his camera along in case he'd see something interesting to photograph. He had received an award for his photo of a fire rescue last month. The photo had been on the front page of the daily paper. Kerry was really proud of her grandfather. But of course, her mom scolded him for getting too close to a fire and endangering himself.

Kerry continued watching as Grampy walked his usual route. She enjoyed the quiet time just watching out the window. As Kerry relaxed, her eyes wandered to a bright light flickering in the vacant house across the street. Hmm, that's odd, Kerry thought. Why is there a light on in the attic of that house? The Cadden family used to live there. But that was years ago. That place had been empty ever since she was a baby. The light continued shining brightly, and Kerry's mind began to race. Who was at the Cadden house?

Kerry hurried downstairs, where her parents were in the den watching the evening news.

"Mom! Dad! There's a light in one of the windows in the Cadden house! I just saw it!" she cried.

"You probably saw the moonlight through the trees, sweetie," her dad said, not taking his eyes off the TV screen. "Nobody is over there. There hasn't been any activity in that old house since Michael Cadden lived there 15 years ago, unless you count the guy who mows the lawn and trims the shrubs. But something tells me he wouldn't be working right now. It's 9:00 p.m."

"No, it was a light. I'm sure it was a light," Kerry said. "Maybe old Michael Cadden came back. Maybe the police were wrong when they thought they found his dead body."

"Babe," her mom said patiently, "we've all heard the story. Michael Cadden murdered two people in that house across the street. In order to escape jail time, Cadden fled the scene of the crime. As he tried to escape the police, his car hit an embankment and burned. Michael Cadden was pronounced dead at the scene. It isn't possible that he's back in his house. I'm sure you saw some sort of optical illusion."

"Can't you at least come upstairs and look for yourselves?" Kerry asked.

Kerry's parents exchanged a smile. There was little Kerry again, engaging in fantasies, like the time she swore she saw a kangaroo in the backyard. It had turned out to be an opossum. Sure, she was just five at the time, but she hadn't changed—not in her parents' eyes anyway.

Her mom walked upstairs and joined Kerry at her bedroom window. "I don't see any light, Kerry," she said.

"Mom, it was there a minute ago. I *know* it was!" Kerry wailed, disappointed that everything was dark now.

"Well, it's nothing to worry about," her mom said, patting Kerry's cheek. "That bad old Michael Cadden burned up in the car wreck. We don't have to worry about him anymore."

Kerry pulled away from her mother's consoling gesture. She didn't want to be patted on the cheek like a five-year-old. "You don't believe me, do you, Mom?"

"Oh, Kerry, let's not go through that again. Let's not have a tantrum. I just know you're a very emotional little girl, and you . . ." her mom began. But Kerry did not want to listen.

"I'm *not* a little girl, and I haven't had a tantrum since I was in kindergarten, Mom!" Kerry was almost screaming now.

"You're having a tantrum right now, darling," Kerry's mom said, raising her eyebrows. "Just go and do your homework and forget all this silliness."

Angrily, Kerry returned to the computer. She hadn't finished the report she had to give on Frederick Douglass. She wouldn't finish it, either. There were several kids giving their report before her in Ms. Creighton's class, and Kerry, most likely, would not have to give hers until the day after tomorrow. So there was no rush.

She was sick of being a good little girl and of bringing home perfect report cards.

Kerry turned on a rap radio station, put on her headphones, and let the pounding sound echo through her angry brain.

More than an hour passed before Kerry finally turned off the music and headed downstairs to eat a late dinner. Even though her mom was a control freak, she was an excellent cook. She used to be a gourmet chef at one of the finest resorts in town, so her family and friends reaped the benefits of her skill.

As Kerry was finishing dinner, Grampy came in the door. "Action over there at the Cadden house, eh?" he asked.

Kerry felt like throwing her arms around her grandfather. He was backing up her story. "See? See?" she cried. "Grampy saw it too. There is something going on over there."

Kerry's mom looked at her father. "Is your coat wet, Dad? It looks wet. I don't want you getting sick," she said.

"My coat's not wet," Grampy said. "It wasn't raining."

Her mom walked over and felt her father's coat to see for herself if it was damp. Kerry felt like screaming. She could see the embarrassment on Grampy's face. There goes her mom again, treating him like a child, Kerry thought.

"Julie," Grampy said, "I think I'm still smart enough to know if it was raining or not. Most creatures can manage that. I may not be as smart as I used to be, but I guess I can manage that much."

"Well, I worry about you," Kerry's mom said. She glanced at Kerry. "Babe, help clear the table. And I don't want to hear any more nonsense about the Cadden house from either of you. Honestly, Dad, you and Kerry are like a couple of little kids!"

2 EVERYBODY IN FOSTER FALLS had heard the story of Michael Cadden. Michael, an inventor, had just finished creating a fuel for automobiles that wouldn't pollute the air. He had put the finishing touches on the fuel and was about to submit the invention for patent. As Michael worked in his basement one evening, he overheard his business partners plotting to steal his invention. Michael flew into a rage and killed both men. He fled the scene quickly, leaving behind the bodies of his partners and a note confessing to the crime.

Michael evaded capture by the police for almost a week, but was spotted at a remote farmhouse in Indigo Lakes, 20 miles south of Foster Falls. When the police arrived, he sped off and led them on a ten-mile chase. They fired shots at his car, causing him to swerve and sail over an embankment. His car exploded into flames. Only charred remains were found in the wreckage.

Since Michael Cadden had no dental records, the identification of the body was difficult. The body was badly burned, and the face was unrecognizable. But the car that was involved was registered under Michael's name, so police believed they were looking at the dead body of Michael Cadden.

....

Kerry stood at her bedroom window again. She stared at the house across the street that had been illuminated earlier that evening. "Could Michael Cadden have come back?" she wondered out loud.

Kerry's mom stuck her head in the doorway. "Kerry, aren't you in bed yet? It's past 10:00. Tomorrow is a school day, you know," she said.

"You're kidding, Mom!" Kerry said in mock confusion. "Since when is Wednesday a school day?"

"Kerry Ann Hoffman, don't take that tone with me. I will not tolerate an attitude, and you know it," her mom said.

"Now go to bed and stop thinking about that man who died 15 years ago."

To herself Kerry said, I'll be all right, Mommy, as soon as I get my teddy bear and my stuffed monkey to sleep with. And, oh, be sure to keep the nightlight on because there might be yellow tigers under the bed. But Kerry knew better than to say those things out loud to her mother, so she replied, "I'll brush my teeth and go to bed."

"All right. Good night, babe," her mom said, satisfied that all was well.

When her mother had gone downstairs, Kerry went down the hall to her grandfather's room. She tapped lightly on the door. "Grampy?"

"Come on in, Kerry," he said.

Kerry went into the room and closed the door behind her. "Grampy, what did you see at the Cadden house tonight?"

Her grandfather shoved his reading glasses to his forehead and said, "The lights were on in the upstairs front bedroom."

"That's what I saw too!" Kerry cried.

"That was the room Michael Cadden used to sleep in," Grampy said.

"How do you know?" Kerry asked, her eyes widening. Her grandfather hadn't lived here at the time of the murders. He had lived with Kerry's grandma in a little beach house in Indigo Lakes. At the time he had been a photographer for the daily newspaper.

"I took some pictures of the house after the murders," he said. He looked much younger than his 78 years when he was talking about his work, back in those days when he had been an important person. Kerry felt so sorry for her grandfather. It was as if once he came to live here, he ceased being a human being to be respected. He was now a foolish old man with symptoms of senility to be cared for by her mother. It seemed he had lost his dignity. "I photographed all the rooms for the police and the paper. The murders happened in that bedroom where we saw the light. He kept a couple of swords in that room, and one was even the murder weapon . . ."

"A sword?" Kerry repeated, feeling weak in the knees.

"Yeah. Michael Cadden was quite an

interesting fellow. He was an inventor, a part-time actor, a sportsman, and a world traveler. He collected stuff from all over the world—masks, swords, different mementos. He was quite accomplished. The murders came as a shock to everybody," her grandfather said.

"You think he really died in that car wreck, Grampy?" Kerry asked. "I mean, they were pretty sure it was him, right?"

Grampy didn't smirk or chuckle at the question like Kerry's parents would have. He didn't put Kerry down for even asking such a question, though it may have been preposterous. "Well, the police found those badly burned remains after the crash. Although they had no dental records to compare the teeth with, they were quite certain they were looking at Michael Cadden. The car that had crashed was registered under his name, and the police did have that note. You know, Michael's confession to committing the crime," he said.

Kerry was impressed at how intelligent and competent her grandfather was. He seemed like a man who could hold his own with anybody, except with Kerry's mom. Around her mom, he was a doddering old man in need of a caregiver, and her mom was all too willing to be the caregiver.

"Well, I hope the police were right. I hope that Michael's body was the body at the scene of the accident. I don't want Michael Cadden coming back," Kerry said.

"Me neither, sweetheart," her grandfather said with a warm smile.

....

In Ms. Creighton's class the next morning, Kerry hoped all the scheduled students would be ready with their reports so her turn wouldn't come up until the next day. She didn't have her Douglass report ready. And not being prepared meant ten points were automatically subtracted from the 100-point project.

Ms. Creighton was a bright young teacher full of enthusiasm. She thought it was a great idea to give each student a Civil War-era person to study and then give an oral report on. Kerry thought it was a stupid idea, because student oral reports were so boring.

Ms. Creighton turned to the first student on her list, "So, Paige, are you ready with your Stephen Douglas report?" Paige Nelson was one of Kerry's best friends, but she wasn't a very good student. Her parents didn't put a lot of pressure on her, so she didn't mind slacking off. "I'm sorry, Ms. Creighton," she said, "I'm not prepared. I couldn't finish my report last night because . . ."

"Don't bother with excuses, Paige," Ms. Creighton cut her off. "You shouldn't have been doing your report at the last minute. I assigned it a week ago. If some disaster struck last night, it should have had no effect on your report. That's ten points deducted from the score you get when you do give the report, Paige. Titus Ramos, are you ready?"

The tall boy got up and delivered a very brief report on Harriet Tubman. He read every word of it, and there were only a few questions afterward. Kerry looked nervously at her watch. She was scheduled to be the fifth student to give a report. Some discussion was supposed to follow every report, so if students asked questions, she might be lucky enough to squeak by without being called upon.

Adam Storm stood up to deliver his report on Charles Sumner. Ms. Creighton smiled in admiration of the young man. He gave a bright, interesting report. The discussion afterward was excellent too. Kerry began to feel safe. There was one more student before her, Lindsay Osborne, and only 20 minutes of class time left. Lindsay was a good student, and her report would likely run long. Kerry breathed a sigh of relief. She could go home tonight and finish her report and be ready tomorrow.

"Lindsay, are you ready to tell us about Andrew Johnson?" Ms. Creighton asked.

Lindsay croaked hoarsely, "I'm sorry, Ms. Creighton, but I have horrible laryngitis. I woke up with it this morning."

Ms. Creighton smiled. "Poor Lindsay. You sound awful. Well, we can't help getting laryngitis, can we? I'll postpone your report. So, let's see, we have time for one more report. Kerry, would you like to tell us about Frederick Douglass?"

Kerry felt like the whole room went black and began swirling around her. She felt like strangling Lindsay Osborne, even though having laryngitis wasn't her fault.

Kerry had done a little work on her Frederick Douglass report and decided to try to fake her way through. "Uh, Frederick Douglass was a really good speaker. He lived during the 1800s, and he spoke against slavery. He made a lot of speeches, and he always said how bad slavery was. Crowds came and listened to him, and he was glad because he wanted to teach them to be against slavery . . ." Kerry stumbled along, sensing she was not impressing Ms. Creighton or anybody else. She hurriedly sat down. Her face felt hot, as if she had a high fever.

"Well," Ms. Creighton said, "are there any questions?"

"Yeah," a boy said, "we don't know much more about Frederick Douglass than we did before Kerry's report."

"Hmm," Ms. Creighton began, "I feel like we are missing a few key pieces of information. Would anyone from the class like to share what they know about

Frederick Douglass?"

"Douglass was a fugitive slave who escaped from a brutal master. He wrote a book about his experiences," Adam Storm said.

"He wrote three books, but the most famous was the *Narrative of the Life of Frederick Douglass*," a girl said, "and that book was as famous as *Uncle Tom's Cabin* in showing people how bad slavery was."

"From what Kerry said, I couldn't even tell if Douglass was black or white," another boy said.

"He was black," Ms. Creighton replied.

The bell rang, and Kerry dashed out of the classroom with Paige. "Oh, Paige," she groaned, "if only you'd been ready with your report, so Ms. Creighton wouldn't have gotten to me."

"I'm sorry," Paige said, "but you weren't ready, either, and that's not my fault."

"Yeah, I know," Kerry said. "Last night was such a weird night. There were lights in that old Cadden house across from us . . . you know, where the murders happened . . ."

"Yeah," Paige said. "I read that the guy

beheaded the men he killed—beheaded them right there in that house! Wow!"

"Beheaded them?" Kerry gasped.

3 KERRY HAD NEVER HEARD or read the details about how the two men had died. Her grandfather mentioned that the murder weapon was a sword—but beheading? Like during the French Revolution when the heads came rolling off the guillotine? "Oh, Paige, that's so gross! Are you sure?"

"Yeah. My older brother has copies of all the newspapers from when it happened. They have all the gory details. I snuck into his room once and read some of them," Paige said.

At the soft drink machine, three girls, including Lindsay Osborne, were getting drinks. They had all bought diet sodas and now were laughing about something.

"That was so clever of you, Lindsay," one of the girls said. "You are too cool."

"Well, what else could I do?" Lindsay said in a perfectly normal voice without a trace of laryngitis. "My boyfriend came over last night, and we watched a funny movie. I didn't have time to finish my report. There was no way I could do a report on Andrew Johnson today, and I knew she wouldn't deduct the ten points if I was sick."

The other girls laughed, but Kerry stomped over. "You cheated! You didn't have to give your report, because you pretended to be sick, so I got my report pushed ahead. Now I've probably flunked because I wasn't ready and gave that stupid fake report. And you weren't even sick. That's not fair!"

Lindsay was a tall, athletic girl, a head taller than Kerry. She was the star of the soccer team. "Stop whining, Kerry. It's not my fault you didn't have your report ready. You should have pretended to be sick too!"

"I could never do that. And now I'm going to get my grade knocked down while you still get the full points," Kerry said. "It's so not fair."

"I'll bet she rats you out, Lindsay," one of her friends warned. "She's going to run to Creighton and explain what happened."

"You better not do that, Hoffman,"

Lindsay said in a sizzling voice. "I have ways of getting even with rats. Trust me."

"I'm not going to tell Ms. Creighton anything, but you're a creep and a cheat," Kerry said.

As Kerry walked away with Paige, Paige said, "Now if somebody else rats her out, you'll get blamed anyway!"

....

After school Mr. Hoffman, who was one of the senior architects in his company, picked Kerry up. He got off work early every day because he set his own hours.

Kerry saw her father coming, wearing his trademark Dodgers baseball cap. He dressed like a 20-year-old. He shopped at the young men's stores, played soccer and tennis with his office team, and frequently beat the younger guys. He looked much younger than his 55 years. "Hey, Sugar Plum," he shouted out of the car as he pulled up.

Two boys standing nearby heard "sugar plum," and they laughed. Kerry's face burned with embarrassment as she scrambled into the car. "Let's GO!" she said.

"How was school?" her dad asked. He always asked that. And he was never satisfied with a brief answer like "fine" or "it was great." He wanted a blow-by-blow account of the whole day.

"It was okay," Kerry said, hoping her dad wasn't in the mood for a long interrogation.

"You seem a little upset, Kerry. Anything happen at school today?" he asked.

"No, everything is fine," she said.

"You know, when your mom and I went to parents' night, we got a pretty good idea of all of your teachers, and they seemed like a good bunch. That Ms. Creighton is a little on the young side, though. How is she doing handling kids not much younger than she is?"

"She's fine," Kerry said. She could tell her father wasn't pleased with the answers he was getting. When they pulled into the driveway and walked in the house, Kerry fled upstairs. But even before she reached the landing she heard her parents talking about her.

"Julie, something is bothering her. I'm

sure of it," Kerry's dad said.

"I've noticed how sensitive she's been lately. She flies off at the least little thing," her mom agreed.

Kerry went to her room and closed the door.

Why did they insist on making her feel like a bug under a microscope? Kerry knew just how a poor bug, skewered on a pin, felt, huge eyes staring down at it . . .

"Look at the thorax . . . is that the right color?"

"See how the little red antennae quiver . . . now what is causing that, do you suppose?"

Kerry did her math homework and a science report. She'd have to work extra hard in history now that she had flubbed the oral report so badly. She worked until dark, then she went to the window to close the blind.

Kerry gasped to see the lights in the bedroom window again. She rushed down to her grandfather's room. He was standing at the window too.

"The lights are on in that window again," he said. "Looks like somebody is living over there now."

"Who could it be? Did that guy Cadden have any relatives?" Kerry asked.

"I'm going to find out what's going on," Grampy said. "I'm going over there and knocking on the door and telling whoever answers that we were concerned to see the lights on. That's just being a good neighbor."

"But what if . . . ?" Kerry felt foolish finishing the sentence.

Grampy smiled. "What if Michael Cadden comes to the door? I don't think so, Kerry. I believe that man died a long time ago," he said.

As her grandfather went downstairs and headed for the door, Kerry's mom called out, "Where are you going, Dad? Dinner's almost ready."

"Be back in a jiffy, Julie," he said.

"But where are you going?" Kerry's mom demanded.

Kerry couldn't believe what she was hearing. Didn't her mom realize what she was doing to Grampy?

"Oh, I believe I see Venus up there and I want to make sure," Grampy lied.

"What?" her mom said. "Oh, Dad, that's silly. Come on, dinner's almost ready."

But the door opened and Kerry's grandfather was gone, with the door firmly closed behind him.

Kerry watched from her bedroom window as her grandfather crossed the street and disappeared behind the thick old pines. You couldn't see the front door of the Cadden house through all of the shrubbery.

Of course, it was ridiculous to believe that Michael Cadden had returned to the place where he had committed a double murder. Kerry knew that. Even if he was alive, which he probably wasn't, he wouldn't return to the scene of the crime.

But still, Kerry found herself trembling. She was anxious for Grampy to get back quickly.

But he didn't come back quickly.

Kerry rushed downstairs and headed for the door.

"Now where are *you* going?" her mom called out. "Honestly, it's enough to drive a person crazy dealing with you and Dad. I'm ready to put dinner on the table, and you two are running around like little children!"

"I'll be right back, Mom. I'm just looking for Grampy," Kerry said.

Kerry ran across the street, following the path her grandfather had taken. She reached the walkway that led to the Caddens' front door and moved slowly down the brick path. As she walked, she glanced up at the gloomy house. It sent shivers of horror through her just to see it, all dark and covered in ivy.

Kerry reached the huge, ornate door. It had the family coat of arms carved into the wood.

Her grandfather was not at the door.

"Grampy?" Kerry called out in a weak voice. She could not believe she was standing at the door to Michael Cadden's house. "Grampy!"

Where could her grandfather have gone? He had to have been here minutes ago. Had he already gone inside? Had whoever was in the house invited him in? Was it possible that he was *forced* inside?

Kerry stepped back from the door, and followed the brick path along the side of the house. She almost stumbled on the overgrown ivy vines lying like green snakes all over. Maybe, she thought, Grampy had rapped on the front door without success and now was checking a side door.

Kerry moved cautiously down the walk. She couldn't see very well. "Grampy?" she called again, growing frightened. All kinds of horrible thoughts entered her mind. Was a madman wielding a sword inside this house?

The images of what had happened here 15 years ago flooded Kerry like scenes from a nightmare. A terrible man swinging a sword. Two men fighting, pleading for their lives.

Maybe Paige had embellished the story. She loved gruesome tales. She loved to tell them to shock other people. She had this crazy book filled with horrible accounts of grisly happenings, like ghosts coming back to wreak vengeance.

Kerry went around the back of the house. There had to be a door there.

Kerry almost screamed when she saw the figure of a man standing at the back door in the darkness. Then she realized it was her grandfather. He turned to her and shrugged. "I've knocked on every door. No one has answered. Kerry, you shouldn't be here. Your mom will strangle us both."

Kerry grabbed her grandfather's hand and said, "Let's go home."

"No, just a minute. I hear somebody in there coming to the door," he said.

Kerry froze. She didn't want to see who might be behind the door.

4 THE DOOR CAME OPEN with a creaking sound. "Yes?" a man asked. He was framed in the doorway—tall and gaunt.

"We're the neighbors from across the street," Kerry's grandfather said. "We were a little concerned to see lights on, because the house has been vacant for a long time. We wanted to make sure everything was okay, that nobody was breaking in. You never know these days . . ."

Kerry could barely see the man, except to notice that he was tall and very thin.

"Everything is all right," the man said. "I'm the owner of the house. I've been away for a long time, but now I've come back to see what I can do about selling the house."

Kerry could see the man's face a little better now. He had a long, narrow face, and small, hooded eyes. He had a beard and a mustache. He looked about 35. That was comforting. Michael Cadden was 40

when he had supposedly died, so if he'd
come back, he would look older than this
man.

"Well, we just wanted to make sure that
nobody broke in," Grampy said. "Sorry to
have bothered you."

"Thank you for your concern," the man
said.

"Yes, well, good luck to you. Oh, I'm
Leo   Poulson,   and   this   is   my
granddaughter, Kerry Hoffman," her
grandfather said. "We live right across the
street."

"I am Aaron Cadden," the man said.
"This used to be my father's house."

Kerry involuntarily shrank back.
Michael Cadden's son! Did he have any
idea that Kerry and her grandfather knew
what had happened in this house?

"Well, good night," her grandfather said.

"Good night, and thank you," Aaron
Cadden said. He closed the door and
Kerry and her grandfather began the walk
home.

"He looks just like his father," Grampy
said. "It's absolutely eerie to look at that
man and remember Michael Cadden. If I

didn't know better, I'd say we were just talking to Michael Cadden himself. The resemblance is that strong."

"But it couldn't be him, could it?" Kerry asked, looking for reassurance.

"No, Michael Cadden is dead," her grandfather said. "Besides, our new neighbor, Aaron, looks like he is in his mid-30s. If Michael *were* still alive, he'd look much older than that.

"Do you think Aaron will stay in that house long? I can't imagine living there, I mean, knowing that people were murdered . . ."

"No," Grampy said. "Aaron will probably sell the house quickly, and the new owners will remodel it. That'll be good for the whole neighborhood. It was gruesome to have the old house there unchanged for so long. Too many memories."

"Yeah, I hope it gets remodeled," Kerry agreed. "You know, Grampy, my friend Paige said those two guys who were killed were beheaded. She read it in a newspaper story. Did that really happen?"

Kerry's grandfather seemed unwilling to

discuss the murders. "Does no good to dwell on the details. That's the stuff of nightmares, and who needs nightmares, right? All I'll say is that the two men were killed in a very decisive manner," he said. "Now, let's hurry up! We're almost home."

....

When they returned home, Kerry's mom was fuming. "Well! It's about time. I was beginning to worry. Dad, I wish you wouldn't wander off like that. My friend Rose's father does that all the time, and once they had to call the police to bring him home," she said.

"That's Mr. Hoskins," Grampy said. "He has serious dementia, Julie. I don't think you need to worry about me so much. I can remember my way home and sometimes I can even remember how to tie my shoes and brush my teeth."

Kerry's mom glared at her father. "You needn't be sarcastic, Dad. You're teaching Kerry bad habits. She's getting an attitude too. Don't forget, Dad, you did have a stroke. That's serious business. You aren't the man you once were, and pretending that you are is just foolish. You had a stroke. A stroke!" she said in a strident voice.

"The way you say it, Julie, I'm almost ashamed of myself for having one," Grampy said. "But my doctor tells me I'm making a full recovery, and I have a very good prognosis. Why don't we look on the bright side?"

Her mom sighed, and Kerry could sense she was getting even more exasperated.

"So where did you two venture off to tonight?" Kerry's father asked.

"We met our new neighbor," Grampy replied.

"Neighbor?" Kerry's mother asked. "We don't have any new neighbors."

"You aren't going to believe it, but it turns out someone is living in the old Cadden house. Remember Michael's son, Aaron? He lives there," Grampy said.

"Interesting," Kerry's father said. "So he was responsible for the lights the other night, I presume?"

"I guess so," Grampy said. "Don't know who else it could be."

"Well, neat," Kerry's mom began. "I had

forgotten Michael had a son. I will have to take a casserole over. You know, as a way to welcome him to the neighborhood. I think that would be nice."

....

At school the next day, Kerry got her grade for the horrible Frederick Douglass report she had given. She got 65 points out of a possible 100—a D! It was the first D Kerry had gotten in her life.

Lindsay Osborne, who had an extra day to work on her report, sweetly told Ms. Creighton that her pesky old laryngitis had gone away. She claimed that orange juice and chicken soup had magically cured her. Lindsay then gave a very good report on Andrew Johnson. Nobody had done better, except for Adam Storm.

"Well, good for you, Lindsay," Ms. Creighton gushed. "You beat the sickness and did a stellar job on the report."

Lindsay smiled. She was sure of an A.

When Kerry was walking outside, she glared at Lindsay. Lindsay came over and cornered Kerry so that her back was against the wall of the physical education building. "One little peep out of you about my feigned illness, and there will be trouble!"

Kerry wasn't planning on trying to make trouble for Lindsay Osborne. But it still angered her that the girl had cheated and gotten away with it. Kerry hurried away to catch up with Vanessa and Paige, and the girls headed for lunch.

"Guess what? Grampy and I met Michael Cadden's son last night," Kerry announced as the girls ate lunch.

"His son?" Paige gasped. "That old murderer had a son? I never knew that! I don't think that was ever mentioned in the newspaper articles I read!"

"Yeah," Kerry said, enjoying the limelight. "My grandfather and I went over there to see why the lights were on, and the son came to the door. His name is Aaron. Grampy said he looks just like his father."

"Weren't you scared?" Vanessa asked.

"Nah," Kerry lied, adding, "well, maybe a little."

"I've seen pictures of the father in the newspaper," Paige said. "And he was really ghastly looking. He had this long gray face and his eyes were hooded like some kind of reptile."

Vanessa knew about the murders at the Cadden house. Nobody could be living in Foster Falls for very long without hearing about it. But she didn't know many of the details. "You guys, why did Cadden kill those men?" she asked.

"They were business partners in some invention, and Michael Cadden thought the other two guys were trying to steal the invention and cheat him," Paige said. "Maybe they were. Who knows? Anyway, it said in the newspaper that he had this old army cavalry sword, and he just whacked at them . . ."

"Ewwww," Vanessa said. "I'm glad I don't live across the street from where that happened!"

"Aaron told us he might sell the house," Kerry said. "Maybe the new owners will tear it down and build a new house. All the other houses on the street, like ours, are much newer. Our house is only like 20 years old, but the Cadden house is maybe 50 years old. It's so ugly and reminds us of the murders."

"Do you think the son knows the whole story?" Vanessa asked.

"I don't know. My grandfather said Aaron looks about 35, so he must have been 20 or something when it happened. Maybe he was away somewhere and didn't even know what was going on until his father was, you know, killed in that accident . . ." Kerry said.

"It must be awful having a father who's a murderer," Vanessa said. "I mean, how do you live that down?"

"It's not his fault," Paige said. "I sort of feel sorry for him."

Richard Greene, a boy sitting at the next table in the cafeteria grinned over at Kerry, Vanessa, and Paige. Richard had asked Kerry out on dates a few times. Each time she told him she wasn't allowed to date until she was at least 16. He was a good-looking boy and Kerry liked him, but he was also a teaser. If he especially liked a girl, he would tease her relentlessly. Now he called out so that everybody could hear, "Look, there's Sugar Plum."

Kerry blushed. He was one of the boys who had heard her dad call her Sugar Plum yesterday. Kerry tried to ignore him, but Richard said in a louder voice, "Hey, Sugar Plum, you having a problem hearing me?"

Vanessa giggled. "Why's he calling you Sugar Plum?" she asked.

Kerry didn't want to admit even to her friends that her father had silly pet names for her. She didn't like to admit, even to herself, how embarrassed she was around her lovable, loud-mouthed, and sometimes immature father. Mr. Hoffman, in his sporty little Audi, acting 20 years younger than he was. He was the oldest dad in the group she hung around in. In many ways he acted the youngest. "I don't know why Richie is calling me that," Kerry said. "I guess he's crazy."

"Daddy picks up his sugar plum every day from school," Richie brayed. "You don't want to let a sugar plum walk home from school by herself. Somebody might pick her up. Sugar plums are very delicate."

Vanessa and Paige laughed at Richard's

antics, but Kerry was getting more angry by the minute. She glared over at Richard and said, "Shut up, Richard!"

"Uh-oh," Richard said in mock concern. "Now I've hurt Sugar Plum's feelings. Poor widdle Sugar Plum."

"He likes you," Paige pointed out. "He's acting stupid because he likes you, Kerry."

"Well, I wish he didn't," Kerry snapped. She left the table and went early to her next class. She was feeling lousy about everything. Her grades were sinking in history, her mom was driving her crazy by watching her like a hawk, and her dad was humiliating her with his silliness. But worst of all, every time she looked out her bedroom window she saw lights in the room where two men had met a gruesome death. It was as if a dark cloud had formed over her and refused to move.

5 "I'M GOING FOR A WALK," Kerry's grandfather announced, just as the sun was going down. "Anybody want to join me?"

"I do all my exercising in dance class," Kerry's mom said. She had an excellent figure, which made her look younger than her years.

"Not me," her dad said. "I've been running around all day at work."

"I'll go," Kerry said.

Her mom's eyebrows shot up. "Don't you have homework, hon?" she asked.

"I finished all my homework," Kerry said. "There wasn't much today."

"Well, all right," her mom said, "but don't stay out too late. It's dangerous walking around at night. You never know who's out there . . ."

When they got outside, Grampy chuckled. "Your mom lives in a scary world, Kerry. When the sun goes down, the gremlins walk."

Kerry laughed heartily. The only chance she got to vent about her mom's strict ways was when she was with Grampy. Kerry's grandfather loved his daughter very much, but he realized she was overprotective.

"I went to the doctor this morning," Grampy said. "He's real pleased with how I'm doing. I might be getting a place of my own in the spring. Might go back to Indigo Lakes where your grandma and I lived right after I retired. Real good fishing there."

Kerry's heart sank. "Oh, Grampy, I'd miss you so much," she said.

"Oh, it's not that far from here. You could catch a bus and be at my place in no time. I love your mom dearly, and your dad is a fine fellow. I'm just not sure I can take much more mothering from my own daughter," he said.

Kerry understood. If she had the chance, she thought she would move too. But still, losing Grampy would be a serious blow. He was her only ally. As if her grandfather could read her mind, he turned and said, "Don't you worry, Kerry.

In a couple of years you'll be off to college."

"Yeah," Kerry said, "but two years feels like forever!"

They walked down their own street, turned right and came up another street. This gave them a side view of the Cadden house. It was not hidden by pine trees on this side, and the large living room window was open to view. It was dusk now, and the lights were already on in the house. There was somebody in the middle of the room who seemed to be dancing around in a strange way.

"What's going on in there, Grampy?" Kerry cried. "What's that guy doing?"

"Looks like Aaron Cadden," Grampy said. "And it appears that he's fencing. Now, isn't that strange? But wait, Michael Cadden fenced in a few movie roles, back in his acting days, so maybe Aaron did too."

"Grampy, is that a sword in his hand?" Kerry asked nervously.

"Yes, they use swords when they fence," her grandfather said.

"But that's so spooky . . . I mean, those

two men were killed with swords . . ."
Kerry said. "What's Cadden's son fooling
around with swords for?"

Unless it isn't Cadden's son, Kerry
thought. Maybe it's Michael Cadden
himself.

"He's probably just reliving his youth,"
Grampy replied.

Kerry shuddered. "Grampy, did you
know either of the men who were
murdered in that house?" she asked.

"Not personally. I knew *of* them. I knew
the families. Michael Cadden was the
oldest of the three inventors. He was kind
of a mentor to the other two. He thought
he was being very generous to let them in
on his invention. I guess he was all the
more infuriated when he thought they
were trying to edge him out of the deal.
They were trying to get a step ahead of
him and beat him to the patent office. I
don't know if all that was true or not, but
one of the men was Archie Folsom, and
the other was Charlie Greene. Greene left
a wife and son, and Folsom was single, I
believe. You might know Charlie Greene,
Jr. His family runs the fried chicken

franchise in town," Grampy said.

Kerry stiffened. "Richard Greene is in my class at school," she said. "He teases me a lot."

Grampy laughed. "Well, if he's bothering you, it must mean he's interested in you, Kerry. The Greenes were a nice family. It was a real tragedy when Charlie was murdered. Charlie, Jr., was finishing college, I believe, and already in the business."

"I suppose Richie never really knew his grandfather, then. If Richie is the same age as I am, it means he was born about a year before the murders," Kerry said. Even though she was mad at Richie, she felt sorry for him because he never got to know his grandfather. She knew how much her grandfather meant to her.

When they got home from their walk, it was dark. They had stopped at the drugstore for ice-cream cones, even though her mom would have totally disapproved of spoiling dinner like that.

"Well, finally!" Kerry's mom said when they walked in. "Where on earth have you been?"

"Just walking and talking, Julie. You have a very unique daughter here. Not many teenagers would want to walk around the neighborhood with their old grandfather and have such good conversation," Grampy said.

Kerry's mom ignored the compliment to Kerry. "I hope you didn't stop off for some junk snack like you did last time. Those snacks spoil your dinner," she said.

Kerry was glad she had wiped her mouth to erase all signs of the chocolate chip cookie dough ice-cream cone. "No, we passed up the corn dogs," Kerry said. On their last walk she and Grampy had had greasy corn dogs. Her mom spent the rest of that evening explaining the health hazards of corn dogs. After the lecture, Grampy had whispered to Kerry, "My goodness, do you think we'll live through the night?" Kerry had giggled wildly, further infuriating her mother.

"We passed the Cadden house," Kerry said. "It was so eerie, Mom. The living room window was open, and Aaron was flying around the room fencing with a sword."

"An *epee*," Kerry's dad said, looking up from his newspaper. "It's called an epee, the weapon one uses in fencing, not a sword, Sugar Plum."

"Dad," Kerry said, "all the kids at school are making fun of me because you pick me up from school and call me Sugar Plum. I wish you wouldn't."

"*All* the kids?" her dad asked with a smirk on his face. "Are you sure every single student at Foster Falls High School is making fun of you, or is it, perhaps, a tiny group of jerks?" Mr. Hoffman was a very smart man. He enjoyed showing it. "When you say *all* instead of *a few* you are guilty of hyperbole. Do you know what that is?"

"Yeah, I know," Kerry said.

"Well, what is it, then?" her dad pressed.

"It's a lie or something," Kerry said.

"No, no. It's an exaggeration to make a point. Remember that. As for curbing my pet names for my beloved daughter out of respect for a couple of dough brains, I can't do that, Kerry-Berry," Kerry's dad said with a wicked grin.

Kerry rolled her eyes. When she was small, she would walk to the park with her father, and along the way he would invent pet names for her. Kerry would squeal with delight at each new invention. She felt like a very special little girl to have so many pet names bestowed upon her by her tall, handsome father. Kerry remembered the names now, and although she once loved them, she now hated them—Curly-girly, Merry-Kerry, Plum Pudding, Pretty Pie, Dimple-doo.

Kerry tried to change the subject. "I think it's horrible that Aaron is fooling around with swords when those men were murdered with swords," she said.

"*Epees*, not swords," her dad corrected her again, as if word usage was more important than murder.

"Well, the men were murdered with a cavalry sword, and the thing in his hand looked like a vicious weapon," Kerry snapped.

"You shouldn't be spying on the neighbors," her mom scolded. "How would we feel if somebody was peering in our front window, watching us? The poor man must feel bad enough, having a father who was a notorious murderer, without nosy neighbors spying on him."

"We weren't spying," Grampy said. "We were just passing by, and seeing this fellow prancing around with a dueling weapon just made us very curious."

"I wish you guys wouldn't walk around at night, anyway," Kerry's mom said. "I talked to Rose today, and they had to search for her dad again. He sneaked down to the Senior Center to play bingo without telling anybody. Rose was just frantic."

"Oh, that old fiend," Kerry's grandfather said. "Imagine playing bingo without getting a permission slip from his daughter. They need to put a bell on him; that's for sure."

"You're trying to be sarcastic again, Dad, and it's not very funny," Kerry's mom said. "Just because Kerry is laughing like a maniac doesn't make it funny. Now Kerry, it seems to me that it's close to your bedtime. Off to bed you go.

"Aww, come on. Ten more minutes? Kerry pleaded.

"Now," her mom replied.

Kerry said her good nights reluctantly, then headed upstairs for bed.

....

The next day, Kerry sat down in history class and glanced at Richard Greene. She had pretty much gotten over being mad at him. And, now that she knew his grandfather was murdered, she even felt a little sorry for him. "Hi," she said.

"Hi," Richard said with a surprised smile.

"Richie, I just found out that the man in the old house across the street from us . . . " Kerry began.

"Yeah, the Cadden house," Richard said.

"Yeah, anyway, your grandfather . . ." she started to say.

"Uh-huh. My grandfather died in that house. Michael Cadden killed him when I was just a baby. My dad told me about it," Richard said, frowning.

"It must have been horrible for your dad to lose his father like that," Kerry said.

"I guess so," Richard said. It hadn't

affected Richard, though, so his sunny smile returned. "Kerry, my sister is turning 18, and her birthday party is at our house on Sunday. We've got a pool, and it'll be lots of fun. You should come."

"I don't know," Kerry said, although secretly, she wanted to go badly. But would that be considered a date? Kerry's mom was very strict about the 16-year-old rule for dating. But then again, would Kerry even have to mention that boys would be there?

6 "CINDY GREENE IS HAVING a birthday party Sunday at her house, and I was wondering if I could go," Kerry said when she got home.

"Isn't Cindy Greene a lot older than you?" her mom asked. "Why would she want you at her party?"

"Uh, well, when I was a freshman she was like my big sister at Foster," Kerry lied. "She helped tutor me in math, and now we are friends." The truth was that Kerry couldn't remember ever seeing Cindy Greene at school.

"Oh, that's nice," her mom said. "Well, if you'd like to go, I'll help you pick up a little gift for her. Your dad can drive you over on Sunday."

"Uh, you know what, Mom?" Kerry said. "Cindy's brother, Richie, he has a car, and he could pick me up and drive me home too."

"And how old is Master Richie?" Kerry's dad asked.

"Oh, he's a junior already," Kerry said.

"I repeat," her dad said with emphasis, "how *old* is Master Richie?"

"Almost 17, or maybe, 17½," Kerry lied. Richard Greene was 16.

"Almost 17? That makes him 16. A 16-year-old driving my Kerry-Berry around town?" her dad said. "I don't think so. I think not, my pretty. If you want to go to the party, your dear old daddy will take you there and pick you up. End of discussion."

Kerry bubbled with resentment, but she didn't say anything. If she made a fuss, her parents would refuse to let her go at all.

On the way over to the Greene house on Sunday morning, Kerry said, "Dad, will you just drop me off and go? I mean, you don't have to hang around and wave to me like it's my first day in kindergarten, okay?"

"My, it must be hard for you to have a father you're so ashamed of," Mr. Hoffman said. "I don't look that bad, do I? I keep fit. I'm a pretty sharp-looking fellow. I make decent conversation. Look, I still have my hair, or most of it."

"It's not that," Kerry mumbled. "It's just that everybody else I know gets to drive themselves to places or go with friends. I'm the only one still getting driven everywhere by my parents, and I feel so stupid! I'm almost 16, and I'm being treated like a six-year-old. Everybody at school laughs at me."

"Here we go again," her dad said. "Everybody at school laughs at you? You mean they all line up on the sidewalk in front of Foster Falls High School and roar with laughter as your mother or I drive up? That must be quite a crowd standing on the sidewalk chuckling away."

Kerry said nothing. Mr. Hoffman pulled to the curb in front of the Greene house, and Kerry scrambled out as fast as she could. Fortunately, there was nobody around to see her.

"Hi, Kerry," Richard said when she walked in. Kerry looked around. All the other people here were older. There was no way in the world Cindy would have invited a 15½-year-old sophomore to her birthday party.

Richard grabbed Kerry's hand and

pulled her through the milling crowd of older people. "Let's get outta here," he said, grinning.

"What you do mean?" Kerry asked nervously.

"I don't know anybody here, and neither do you," Richard said. "They're all Cindy's friends. Guys here in their 20s! Let's jump in my pickup and go somewhere else."

"I can't," Kerry said. "My parents don't let me ride with 16-year-olds."

"How are they going to know? We'll just drive down to the Zany Zone, play some games, and have pizza. What's wrong with that?" Richard asked.

Kerry hesitated. She'd never disobeyed her parents in such a big way before. But they were so unreasonable! She didn't get to do half of what her friends could do. "I don't know, Richie," she said.

"Awww, Kerry, if you don't start acting independent, you'll turn into a freak. What your parents don't know won't hurt them. We'll just stay at the Zany Zone for a couple of hours. Then I'll take you back to the house, and you can call your father to come pick you up. There's nothing wrong with doing that," Richie pleaded.

"Okay, Richie," Kerry finally said, following him to his pickup. The Zany Zone had pool tables, video games, and air hockey. Plus, it had ice cream, pizza, and loads of candy. There was even a splash area where you could cool down by jumping into fountains.

Kerry and Richie saw lots of kids from Foster Falls High at the Zany Zone. That made Kerry very nervous. What if somebody told on her?

Suddenly, Lindsay Osborne walked up to Kerry. "You little rat!" Lindsay hissed.

"What are you talking about?" Kerry demanded.

"You *know* what I'm talking about! Ms. Creighton called me in and said I'd lied about having laryngitis. Now, instead of an A, I've got a D. You were the one who ratted me out!"

"I wasn't," Kerry insisted. "I never said a word."

"Liar! You were so mad that I got a good grade, and you didn't, that you had to get even with me," Lindsay said.

"A lot of kids heard you talking in a normal voice that day you claimed to have laryngitis," Kerry cried. "Anybody could have told Ms. Creighton you were faking."

"Well, nobody else had a reason to make trouble for me," Lindsay said. "All I can say is, you'll be sorry for doing that." And she walked away.

"Oh, wow," Kerry groaned. "If she tells my parents that I'm here, I'll be grounded for the rest of my time in high school!"

"Does she know that you're not supposed to be here?" Richard asked.

"Everybody knows how strict my parents are! I'm not allowed to date at all, and you and me being here looks like a date," Kerry said.

After a while Kerry got distracted playing a video game, and then she and Richard bought some ice cream. But Kerry still couldn't get Lindsay off her mind. Lindsay seemed really angry, despite Kerry's reassurance that she had not told Ms. Creighton about the fake illness.

Kerry and Richard were coming out of

the Scary Maze laughing, when Kerry gasped.

"Well, what a surprise," Kerry's dad said grimly. "This doesn't look like the Greenes' birthday party, but here you are, Kerry."

"Dad . . . I . . . I mean, we just came here for a little while," Kerry said. "We weren't doing anything . . ."

"Young lady, I am shocked beyond words that you would deliberately deceive us like this," her dad said.

Lindsay was standing nearby, smiling.

Richard was flushed and nervous. "I'm sorry, Mr. Hoffman. It was, uh . . . my fault. Kerry wanted to stay at the birthday party, but I talked her out of it. It wasn't her fault," he said.

"On the contrary," Mr. Hoffman said. "It *was* my daughter's fault. It was 100 percent Kerry's fault. She knew the rules. She knew she wasn't supposed to do something like this, and she did it anyway."

A few kids Kerry knew were standing there listening to her humiliation. They were enjoying the show. Kerry was on fire with embarrassment when her father reached out, firmly took her hand, and marched her down the sidewalk leading from the Zany Zone.

"I just can't believe you did this," Kerry's dad said as they neared the parking lot.

"What did I do?" Kerry cried. "I just came to this stupid place with a classmate!"

"If you wanted to come here, your mother or I would have brought you," her dad said. "But instead, you lied and said you were at a birthday party, so some underage boy could drive you here."

Kerry climbed into the Audi, and her father closed her door.

"You made a fool of me in front of 50 kids," Kerry stormed. "I'll never live it down."

"Good," her dad said. "I hope you were embarrassed down to your little painted toes, my dear!"

How dare you do this to me! Kerry thought silently. How dare you treat me like this! I'll never forgive you for this!

When Kerry walked into the house, her

mother was standing there like an avenging angel, her arms folded. She glared at Kerry.

"I found her with Richard at the Zany Zone," Mr. Hoffman said, making it sound really grave, like Kerry had been caught shoplifting from the jewelry store. And all she had done was go to the Zany Zone with Richard in the middle of a Sunday afternoon!

"Kerry Ann Hoffman, how could you lie to us like this?" her mom asked in an emotional voice. "When I got that phone call that you were with Richard at that amusement park, I was absolutely astonished."

Boiling hot tears ran down Kerry's face. It wasn't fair. Nobody Kerry knew was treated like this.

"I didn't do anything!" Kerry screamed. "You're both so unfair. You treat me like a criminal! I feel like I live in juvenile hall. Why don't you buy handcuffs and make me wear them? Why don't you put bars on my windows?"

"Are you done?" Mrs. Hoffman asked coldly. "If you are, then you can go to your room and think about what you've done. We'll talk to you later when you can behave in a calm, civilized manner."

Kerry ran up the stairs to her room. She was ready to fling herself on her bed and cry her eyes out when she noticed that her computer was gone. Her radio was gone. Her phone had been unplugged and taken away. Her CD player was nowhere in sight.

Kerry stood there shaking. She went to the window to get some air, and then she saw him. Aaron Cadden was standing down there on the sidewalk. He seemed to be staring up at Kerry's window. It was her first really good look at the man. His face was sallow and his cheeks caved in. He looked like a cadaver. His eyes peered from hollow caverns.

He didn't look 35. He looked much older. He looked almost 60. Like Michael Cadden would look if he were still alive . . .

7

KERRY TURNED AROUND and ran downstairs. "He's out there on the sidewalk looking up at my window!" she screamed.

"Kerry," her mom said in a grim, calm voice, "you will do anything to distract us from what happened today, won't you? Well, it won't work."

"Mom, he's down there looking up at my window! I swear he is. It's that Cadden guy!" Kerry screamed.

Kerry's mom walked to the living room window. She opened the curtains. "I don't see anyone. What a surprise!" she said.

"Mom, he was there just two seconds ago. I guess he saw me at the window and went away. He didn't want to be caught looking at our house, but it was him! He looked old and awful, like the walking dead or something!" Kerry said.

Kerry's dad joined them. "Kerry, stop it," he said in a firm voice. "Just stop it. Go back to your room and think about what you did today."

Kerry returned to her bedroom, crushed. She had to talk to somebody. She felt so alone. She needed a shoulder to cry on—Vanessa Bassett. She had to call Vanessa. She was Kerry's closest friend and she would help . . .

She turned and reached for the phone. Then suddenly, she remembered it had been confiscated. Kerry walked down the hall and called softly at her grandfather's room. "Grampy?"

He didn't answer.

Oh no, Kerry thought, even Grampy is against me now. My only ally, and now he's turned against me too.

"Grampy, please. I need to talk to you," Kerry cried in a louder voice, beating on his door.

Mrs. Hoffman started up the stairs. "Kerry, don't think you can cry on your grandfather's shoulder now. He isn't home, for one thing. And even if he were home, he wouldn't side with you in something as serious as this. You defied us," her mom said. "If you don't like what's happened to you, then make up your mind to earn our trust back. Then you'll get your things back. In the meantime, if you need the computer for school, you may use the one in the family room."

Kerry cast her mother a bitter look and returned to her room. She was afraid to look outside, for fear the awful-looking man was standing there again. Kerry crawled into bed and pulled the blankets up over her head and tried to sleep. She slept fitfully, her head full of nightmares. In her dreams, Michael Cadden was climbing up the side of her house and peering in her window. She tried screaming until her throat ached, but nobody heard her. Michael continued climbing in the window, sword in hand. Then Kerry woke up, shaking. She didn't sleep for the rest of the night.

In the morning, as Kerry ate her oatmeal, her mom said, "I haven't heard an apology from you yet, Kerry."

"I'm sorry," Kerry snapped.

"That's not good enough. You know you don't mean it. You know it was wrong to sneak off with Richard, but you're too stubborn to admit it," Kerry's mom said.

There was no conversation in the car as Mrs. Hoffman drove Kerry to school. Kerry ran from the car, eager to see her friends, and at last, share her misery with someone.

Before history, Kerry caught up to Vanessa. She grabbed her friend's arm and poured out what had happened on Sunday. "Now I'm grounded, and all my stuff is gone. It's so horrible. I've been cast into prison in my own home, and that monster across the street is getting closer! Last night he was standing on the sidewalk looking up at our house, but nobody will believe me. Mom and Dad hate me!"

"Throw yourself on their mercy," Vanessa suggested. "Get all weepy, and say you're sorry. Parents really fall for that. You'll see. They'll forgive you in a heartbeat, and everything will be okay again."

"But Van, I didn't do anything wrong! I mean, I bet *your* parents wouldn't mind if you went to the Zany Zone on a Sunday afternoon with a boy from school," Kerry said.

"My parents are pretty cool," Vanessa said. "They're really young. Mom's only 33, and she acts like a kid. I think she's afraid of disciplining us kids about anything."

"My parents are old," Kerry said. "They don't even remember being kids themselves."

"But still, the only way to get your stuff back is going mushy, girl," Vanessa said.

At lunchtime, Kerry ate with Vanessa and Paige. They were talking about Michael Cadden and the murders when Kerry spotted Richard Greene standing nearby. He looked forlorn. Kerry had gotten into all that trouble because of him, but she didn't hate him for it. He didn't mean any harm. And when he'd suggested sneaking off to the Zany Zone, Kerry wanted to go as much as he did. So Kerry smiled at him and invited him over.

"You know what, you guys?" Kerry said. "My grandfather thinks our neighbor, Aaron, looks about 35, but I don't. He looks ancient. I'm not convinced that the guy is really Aaron. Something tells me he might be Michael."

"But Michael Cadden burned up when

the police were chasing him 15 years ago," Richard said. "The police chased him through the hills and shot at his car. They found the bullet in the burned remains. My dad told me about it. He said, 'Rich, the fellow who killed your grandpa had a fiery death. That was justice.' That's what my dad told me."

"My grandfather said there weren't any dental records for Michael Cadden, so they couldn't check that against the dead guy," Kerry said. "I'm telling you guys, it's got to be Michael over in that house. I can feel it in my blood. I get goosebumps just thinking about it."

"Wow," Paige said. "If that's true, then there's a double murderer living across the street from you. If I were you, I wouldn't sleep a wink at night. I'd be afraid. I'd be so afraid. I mean, like, if you're sure it's Michael Cadden living over there, then why don't you call the police? If he didn't die in that car crash 15 years ago, then they have to arrest him now. They can do that. You can arrest somebody for murder, no matter how long ago they did it. That's the law."

"I think you're wrong, Kerry," Vanessa said. "The son just looks old and ugly, but he's probably only about 35. Some people look really old even when they're not."

"Hey, I know," Paige said suddenly, "I'll get those old newspapers from my brother's room. I'll bring them to school tomorrow, and you can look at the photos of Michael Cadden. I remember seeing a couple of photos of him. Then you'll know if the guy who says he's the son really is the son."

"Yeah, or if he's actually the father. That's a great idea," Kerry said, but deep down in her heart she wasn't all that eager to have her worst fears confirmed. She hoped that the photographs would prove her suspicions wrong.

When Kerry walked into her history class, Lindsay caught her at the door. Lindsay smirked in Kerry's direction and whispered, "How are things at your house, rat? Pretty hot, huh? Too bad."

A wave of throbbing hatred went through Kerry. She hated Lindsay so much at that moment that it made her sick to her stomach. It was almost frightening to feel so much hatred. It felt like there was a monster inside of her, occupying her body. All kinds of revolting forms of revenge against Lindsay paraded through her mind, and she relished each one of them.

If only a snake would crawl into Lindsay's bed. If only a big, hairy spider would hide in her hairbrush and jump out at her when she tried to comb her hair. If only she would fall into a manhole and never get out.

It dawned on Kerry, as she sat contemplating revenge against Lindsay, that old Michael Cadden must have felt like this when he learned his business partners were trying to cheat him. Or at least when he believed they were trying to cheat him. Kerry didn't like the feelings she was having. Was it this easy to become a monster?

When Kerry's father came to pick her up that day, he did not call her Sugar Plum. He just pulled up in the Audi and sat there silently as she got in. Kerry almost longed for all the stupid times when her father did call her Sugar Plum. It was better than silence!

As the Audi moved from the curb, Kerry said, "I'm sorry, Dad. I shouldn't have let Richie drive me to the Zany Zone. It was wrong and stupid of me." Kerry wasn't trying to follow Vanessa's advice by doing a 'so sorry' act. She really was sorry. Even though her parents were strict, she loved them, and she knew they loved her.

"That's right," her dad said. "You know, if we didn't love you so much, we wouldn't make all these rules and be on your case all the time. We just couldn't bear it if something bad happened to you. I hope you know we're coming from love . . ." her dad's voice shook a little with emotion. Kerry was surprised to hear that. Maybe, she thought, her dad felt bad all over, just like she did. Maybe he felt as miserable as she did to have this anger between them.

"I just wasn't thinking, Dad," she said. "I'm really sorry, though."

"Well, good. The next time somebody suggests doing something like that, maybe you won't do it," Kerry's dad said. Just before they turned off on their street, he said, "What a hot day this has been. Think we should grab an ice-cream cone before we go home?"

"Yeah, that'd be great," Kerry said. She knew her mom wouldn't approve, but as long as her dad was in this mood, it was okay.

Kerry and her father sat in a booth eating their ice-cream cones. "Dad," Kerry said, "last night I did see that Cadden guy down on the sidewalk looking up at our windows. Honestly I did."

Mr. Hoffman licked around his cone carefully. Then he looked at Kerry and said, "Yeah. I'm sorry we didn't believe you. He was outside our house earlier this morning too. We called the police and alerted them. There's something wrong with that man. It's got me worried. It's really got me worried . . ."

8 THE NEXT DAY at school, Kerry, Vanessa, and Paige gathered around the yellowed newspapers that Paige had gotten from her brother's room. The photograph from the 15-year-old newspaper seemed to stare back at them.

"Well," Paige demanded, "is it the guy you saw in the house across the street, Kerry?"

Kerry frowned. "It looks a lot like him, but I'm not sure. My grandfather said the guy claiming to be the son looks just like his father. I just have this creepy feeling that Michael Cadden has come back to his house and that he's over there right now. I just don't think that guy who says he's Aaron really is Aaron," she said.

As the girls looked at the newspaper, Kerry spotted Lindsay and her boyfriend sitting on a short brick wall, talking. Lindsay had placed her purse beside her, and now, it had slipped into the thick ivy behind her.

"Hey, look. There's Lindsay and her boyfriend," Kerry said. "She's so wrapped up in him that she didn't even notice her purse fell over the wall."

"Look," Vanessa said excitedly, "she's getting up and walking away with her boyfriend! She forgot her purse. Isn't that incredible? She doesn't even realize she doesn't have her purse with her!"

Paige started giggling. "Wow, that is so funny. Look, Kerry, she's going to get to class and remember her purse isn't with her and she'll freak out. That happened to me once. I almost lost it. I mean, my whole life was in that purse—my ID, my makeup, money, everything!" she said.

"Oh," Kerry said excitedly, "it couldn't be happening to a better person. She so deserves bad luck after what she did to me. Ratting me out to my parents when I didn't even tell Ms. Creighton that she lied and cheated!"

Lindsay joined hands with her boyfriend as they walked slowly toward the first class of the day. They were talking and laughing together, oblivious to those around them.

"It's the most horrible feeling in the world when you discover your purse is gone," Paige said.

"Yes! Yes!" Kerry cried. "Lindsay drives a car, so her car keys and her driver's license are in the purse too. Can you imagine her terror when she finds it's all gone?"

"Probably a credit card too," Paige laughed. "Oh boy, is she in for it."

Vanessa, Paige, and Kerry laughed as Lindsay moved farther and farther from her purse, which now lay hidden in the ivy next to the brick wall she had been sitting on.

"She'll never, in a million years, think to look there," Kerry said. "She'll be running around the classroom like a headless chicken, looking for her purse."

"I hope some goody-two-shoes doesn't find it by accident and return it to her," Vanessa said. "That would be a shame."

"There's a lot of stealing that goes on at this school," Paige said. "If somebody finds it, they'll probably steal the money from it, and throw the purse in the trash."

Paige and Vanessa went off to the

restroom, but Kerry remained, staring at the brick wall and the ivy where Lindsay's purse nestled. Kerry's heart was pounding with joy. A misfortune had befallen Lindsay, who so richly deserved it. The fates had dealt her a blow. Lindsay had spitefully made trouble between Kerry and her parents, and now she was about to be punished.

Lindsay disappeared around a corner with her boyfriend.

Yes! Kerry exulted to herself. She wanted to stay here a few more minutes to see what happened. Class didn't start for seven minutes, and she had time.

Kerry was sitting on a bench a few yards from the social studies building. She looked down in her lap to discover she still had Paige's manila envelope with the newspaper accounts of the Cadden murders. She pulled out one of the yellowed articles and began reading.

Murderer Leaves Note Explaining Crime

Hmm, Kerry thought. This must be the confession that was found in the Cadden house! She continued reading.

They were going to ruin me. I did nothing but good for them, yet Greene and Folsom were out to get me. I hated them with every sinew of my being. I killed them because they deserved it. I killed them. I alone, with help from no one else. I, Michael Cadden, have rid the world of two evil men.

Kerry shuddered. Michael Cadden wanted there to be no mistake that he had committed the crime. He had fled the scene, but the confession in the note would have doomed him. It was almost as if he was proud of his wicked deed, and he wanted all the world to know of it.

Kerry could understand how the man felt. He had taken down his enemies, and he exulted in it. Just like Kerry was exulting in Lindsay's impending misfortune.

Kerry finally went to her class where Lindsay was at her desk, in hysterics.

"My purse! Where's my purse?" she was screaming.

Kerry sat down. Oh, this is rich, this is so rich, she thought. Look at her squirm!

"You guys, I had my purse when I came in," Lindsay cried. "What happened to it?"

"Are you sure you brought it into class?" Ms. Creighton asked. "You didn't leave it in the restroom, did you?"

"I always keep it on my shoulder," Lindsay said. "I take it off when I sit down here and stick it under the desk."

She had forgotten putting the purse beside her on the wall when she was talking to her boyfriend.

Oh, yes, YES! Kerry thought, remembering the terrible feeling she'd gotten when her dad appeared at the Zany Zone that Sunday afternoon. And the anguish she had felt when she had discovered her phone, TV, computer, even her radio had been taken from her room. How much she had suffered from her mom's cold anger! It was all Lindsay's fault, and now she was getting it back. The tables had turned. It was simple justice, all the more sweet, since Kerry had taken no action to cause it.

"You guys," Lindsay cried, "I had a hundred dollars in that purse. A hundred dollars! I was supposed to pick up Dad's prescription from the drugstore on the way home from school. I can't lose that money!"

Kids began searching around the room—looking under desks and behind bookcases.

Kerry started to tremble. Seeing Lindsay suffer had given her great satisfaction for a few minutes, but now another emotion was kicking in—guilt.

Somebody's prescription wouldn't be filled. Maybe it was important medication. Kerry didn't know what was wrong with Lindsay's father, but maybe it was serious . . .

"You didn't have your purse when you came into class today," Kerry said in a faltering voice.

Lindsay turned sharply. "What? I did too! I always keep my purse with me," she said.

"You were sitting on the brick wall out there with some guy," Kerry stammered, her lips numb. "Maybe you left your purse there."

"Ohhh!" Lindsay screamed. She went tearing out of the classroom, running all the way to the wall. She dug frantically in the ivy and uncovered her purse just as she left it. Then she came running back into the classroom, clutching her purse to her chest. "Oh, thank goodness! I found it! I don't know what I would have done. I'm so glad . . ." Her voice trailed. She turned to look at Kerry. She tried to say something, but the words seemed to be stuck in her throat. With some effort she got them out. "Thanks, Kerry. You saved my life," she finally said.

Kerry didn't know what she felt, but the rage she had been feeling earlier seemed to seep out of her like poison leaving a wound. She felt better.

....

At lunch, Kerry read through more of the articles about the Cadden murders. There was tragic detail. Mr. Greene had left a wife and son. Mr. Folsom left grieving parents. From their photographs in the paper, they looked like nice, young, pleasant-looking men. They didn't look like the evil thieves Michael Cadden described. But who knew for sure? Looks can be deceiving.

Kerry glanced at the photographs of the house, and then she gasped at the name of the photographer—L. Poulson. But then, she thought, she shouldn't be surprised.

Her grandfather had told her he'd taken photographs at the scene of the crime. He worked for the *Foster Falls Tribune* at the time.

Finally Kerry got to the last article. It described the chase that led to Michael Cadden's fiery death. The headline of the story caught her eye.

Local Photographer Gives Tip Leading to Murderer

Leo Poulson, local photographer, was scouting for property in Indigo Lakes when he spotted Michael Cadden, wanted for a double murder in Foster Falls. Poulson had taken extensive photographs of the Cadden home and he was familiar with Michael Cadden. Poulson saw him at a remote farmhouse and called police. By the time police arrived, Cadden was fleeing in his car, but police took chase, shooting Cadden, and causing his car to leave the road in a fiery crash.

Kerry turned numb. Grampy had never told her he was the one who fingered Michael Cadden. He never said he'd tipped the police.

But what if Michael Cadden had somehow escaped that fiery crash? What if he was riding with another person, and he had been thrown clear of the accident, landing unhurt in the brushy ravine? What if Michael Cadden had now returned to Foster Falls to wreak vengeance on the man who had turned him in?

When Mr. Hoffman picked Kerry up she told him what she had learned. "Dad, did you know Grampy was the one who told the police where Michael Cadden was hiding 15 years ago?" she asked.

"Yeah, I knew that. I never gave it much thought, though. The police claimed Michael was killed, so it didn't seem important," he said.

"But isn't it possible that Michael wasn't killed? That somebody else was in the car that day? Dad, I'm scared of that guy across the street, whoever he is," Kerry said. "I don't want anything to happen to Grampy."

Kerry's dad frowned. "I think it's time I made a trip to the police department."

9 "HOW COME YOU NEVER told me you were the one who spotted Michael Cadden and put the police on his tail, Grampy?" Kerry asked at dinner that evening.

"I didn't see it as a big deal," her grandfather said. "I did what any good citizen would have done. After all, the man was wanted for a double murder."

"Maybe he's back now for revenge," Kerry said.

Grampy smiled. "No, Michael Cadden is dead. As for his son, he's an odd one to be sure, but he must know that what his father did 15 years ago was awful. I'm sure he wouldn't want to settle any scores on behalf of his father," he said.

"But, Grampy, he might want to avenge his father's death. I mean, it's possible. Like, it's even possible the father somehow got away that day, and he's living across the street!" Kerry insisted.

"Kerry, don't worry about it," Grampy said.

"But that guy over there is practicing with his swords and stuff," Kerry said.

"Kerry, murder isn't a hereditary trait. Murder is a very rare thing, fortunately. I don't think I've ever heard of a father murdering someone and then his son becoming a murderer too. I would think such a terrible tragedy in Aaron Cadden's family would turn him even more against violence," her grandfather said.

"Well, Dad is going to talk to a friend down at the police department and ask him to just keep an eye on the Cadden house. It scares me that the guy— whoever he is—was standing on the curb looking up at the window," Kerry said.

"Well, I guess it can't hurt to keep the police department informed," her grandfather replied.

On Saturday morning, Mrs. Hoffman told Kerry that she and Mr. Hoffman were going to her sister and brother-in-law's house for dinner. They were celebrating a promotion Mrs. Hoffman's brother-in-law had just received. "Your dad and I will be gone until about midnight tonight. I'm sure you and your grandfather can hold down the fort, Kerry."

Grampy looked up from the magazine he was reading and said, "We'll do our best."

"I've got a lot of homework to do," Kerry said.

"Remember, Kerry," her mom said, her eyes narrowing, "no monkey business. I haven't completely forgotten that afternoon at the Zany Zone, babe. No calling Richie to come over or anything, right?"

"Oh, Mom!" Kerry said, hurt that her mother was still hitting her over the head with that mistake. Couldn't she get over it? After all, it was the *first* time Kerry had ever pulled something like that.

"Don't 'Oh Mom' me," Mrs. Hoffman said sternly. "When your grandfather goes out for his walk, you might just try to sneak some friends over. Well, don't even think about it."

"You know I wouldn't do that," Kerry said. "I mean, I told you guys I was sorry about what happened!"

"I can't rely on your grandfather to keep an eye on you. He'll take his walk, come home, and doze in the chair," her mom said.

"Or, I might get lost on my walk and never come home at all, like poor Mr. Hoskins," Grampy said in a sarcastic voice.

Kerry's mom cast her father an annoyed look. Then Mr. Hoffman came in. "Well, I had a chat with Jules Chapman, my police friend, and he did some checking on Aaron Cadden. He assured me that the guy in the house across the street really is Aaron Cadden. Michael's father really died in that car crash. I know there was some question at the time, but more tests were conducted on the dead body, and it was Michael Cadden, the man who murdered those two fellows. That should make us all breathe a little easier. There is no murderer living across from us. Unless, of course, we want to believe Michael Cadden's ghost is the one over there." Mr. Hoffman chuckled to himself.

Kerry didn't think it was a laughing

matter. Paige had told her a lot of horror stories about evil spirits wreaking havoc. Of course, she didn't believe the stories, but still, they caused her to question.

"I felt sure, right from the start, that it was the son, Aaron," her grandfather said. "I knew Michael Cadden quite well. One time he was the judge of the town rose garden contest, and I took a lot of pictures of him."

"The judge of a rose garden contest?" Kerry's mom gasped. "That violent man?"

"People are a contradiction," Kerry's grandfather said. "Michael Cadden loved roses. His whole yard used to be full of them. His wife hated the roses."

"When did she die?" Mrs. Hoffman asked.

"Oh, she didn't die. They were divorced for a long time. She left Michael Cadden and took Aaron across the country to live in New York. Broke Michael Cadden's heart. He consoled himself with roses and his Persian cat," her father answered.

"How could such an apparently nice, normal man have committed such a crime?" Mrs. Hoffman wondered aloud.

Kerry's grandfather shrugged. "Everyone who knew him was very shocked," he said. "Cadden was a shy man. Brilliant yet reclusive."

....

Kerry's parents left for dinner at 7:00, and Kerry and her grandfather had salad and a casserole. There was peach pie for dessert.

"You know, Grampy," Kerry said, "there's a girl at school who made a lot of trouble for me, and I hated her a lot. I was wishing for horrible things to happen to her, and then it dawned on me that hating somebody like that made me feel sort of like a monster . . ."

Her grandfather nodded. "That's right. There's a bit of a monster in all of us, and we've got to keep it under control," he said.

"This girl, I saw her lose her purse, and she was all worried and stuff, and I was enjoying it. But then I felt guilty, so I told her where her purse was. She thanked me, and the hate drained out of me, like someone had pulled a plug," Kerry said.

"Good for you," her grandfather said. "I'm proud of you."

"Too bad Michael Cadden didn't stop and think before he killed those men, huh, Grampy? He must have had a good side if he grew flowers and had a cat."

"Probably so. Feel like a walk, Kerry?" he asked.

"I don't think so. I've got a whole chapter in history to study. We've got a big test coming up, and a lot hangs on this test," Kerry said.

"Okay, then," Grampy said. "I'll go around the block and be back shortly."

A tiny current of fear ran through Kerry. Should she be afraid? she wondered. Afraid for her grandfather? For herself alone in the house? Should she be afraid of Michael Cadden's son across the street?

"It's pretty dark outside," Kerry said. "Maybe you shouldn't take a walk. It's kinda scary out there . . ."

Her grandfather laughed. "Don't tell me you're getting like your mother! Talk about scary! Living with two mothers, now that's frightening! I've taken walks all my life, in Asia, Africa, South America, and nobody ever bothered me. I'm not about to stop now," he said.

"But you know, that guy across the street," Kerry muttered. "I mean, he *is* weird."

"I'll be okay, Kerry," her grandfather said. "The police checked him out. He is who he says he is. He's not a murderer come back from the ashes. He's just the unfortunate son of a very disturbed man. I'm sure Aaron Cadden is a very pleasant fellow, once you get to know him. He probably doesn't have the slightest idea that I called the police on his father. That's ancient history now. All he probably wants to do is sell the house and get on with his life."

"Okay," Kerry said. She watched her grandfather slip on a sweater and head out on his walk.

Kerry sat down at her desk and studied history for about an hour, then she called Paige. "Things are getting better around here," Kerry said. "I have my phone back. Isn't that great?"

"Yeah," Paige said. "Your parents home?"

"No, they went out to dinner. It's just me and Grampy. But he's out walking now," Kerry said.

"Wow, didn't you say that weird guy across the street lurks around your house?" Paige asked. "I mean, aren't you afraid of being alone in the house?"

"No," Kerry lied. She would give anything to have her grandfather home with her. "The police checked the guy out, and they said it really is Aaron Cadden living across the street from us."

"I don't know, Kerry. In this book I have, it tells about Blackbeard, that famous pirate from the old days. Well, he was beheaded, and his body vanished in the water by Cape Hatteras. But that wasn't the last of him. Lots of people saw him after that, coming ashore at night and stomping around," Paige said.

"Come on, Paige. I don't need to hear this," Kerry groaned.

"Well, I'm just saying to be careful. I mean, you ought to be afraid sometimes. It's foolish to be too brave," Paige said.

"Well, Grampy will be home any minute now," Kerry said. "He's usually gone about

30 minutes, and it's been, hmmm . . .
longer than that. He should be back
soon . . ."

Kerry stared at the clock. She hadn't
realized, until this moment, that her
grandfather had been gone almost an hour
and ten minutes!

Kerry felt uneasy when she hung up.
She went to her bedroom window and
looked out into the night. Usually, when
her grandfather came back from one of
his walks, she could see him coming. The
street lights were bright enough to
illuminate even someone at the end of the
street walking on the sidewalk.

But she didn't see him coming.

Kerry started worrying. What if Grampy
fell on a crack in the sidewalk and hurt
himself? He *was* 78 years old, and he'd
had that stroke.

Stop it, Kerry scolded herself. She was
getting like her mom now, and she didn't
ever want to do that.

But there was still no sign of her
grandfather, and it was getting late.

10 I SHOULD HAVE GONE with him, Kerry told herself. I could have taken the time to walk, and studied afterward. Why didn't I go with him?

Another five minutes passed, and there was still no sign of her grandfather. Maybe he ran into an old friend and they'd gotten lost in conversation, Kerry reasoned. Grampy was not very good at noticing how much time had passed. He always said all those years he worked he was chained to a clock. But now he's retired, and he doesn't have to be clock-bound.

Grampy might have even stopped at the drugstore for a cup of coffee.

Kerry was tempted to call her parents and tell her mom that her grandfather was late. But she didn't want to rat him out like Lindsay had ratted her out. Kerry and her grandfather had an understanding that they would respect each other.

Kerry grabbed her light jacket from the

closet and ran downstairs. She would take the route her grandfather walked, and surely she would run into him before long. He would probably resent that she'd come looking for him, but she could invent some excuse about wanting to take a walk after all. Kerry had to make sure he was all right.

Kerry set out on the route she often went with her grandfather. They usually went around the whole block, including the little mini-mall at the corner where they stopped for ice cream.

The street seemed unusually quiet and spooky. There was no moon, and even the warm glow of the street lights seemed dim in the light fog.

Kerry walked quickly, hoping to meet her grandfather before she went very far. She rehearsed what she would say. Oh, hi, Grampy. I really needed a walk tonight too. That was a big dinner, and I had two slices of peach pie! I wanted to walk off some calories. Of course, her grandfather would see right through the ploy. He would take one look at Kerry's worried face, and the lie would be exposed.

Kerry became more worried the farther she went. When she reached the mini-mall, she went in the drugstore. "Nope," the clerk said, "no sign of your grandfather."

Kerry made up her mind that if she walked the whole distance and arrived home without seeing her grandfather, she would have no choice but to call her parents. Kerry hated the thought of doing that, but she would have to.

She continued to walk, turning onto the street that marked the midway point. Soon, she would pass the Cadden house, and she dreaded that.

Kerry was breathing hard as she neared the old house. A hundred terrors went through her mind. What if her grandfather was passing the house on his way home, and Aaron Cadden had forced him into the old house? Maybe he was being held prisoner!

As she walked past the Cadden house, Kerry slowed down. She listened for any strange sounds.

If she heard moans or groans, Kerry was sure she would start screaming.

"Kerry!" came a harsh whisper.

Kerry almost jumped out of her skin, before she realized her grandfather was crouching in the shrubbery alongside the Cadden house. "Grampy! What are you doing here?"

"Shhhh," Grampy said. "Listen!"

Kerry was shaking so much that she grabbed her grandfather's hand for support. Soon she heard the sounds that were coming from inside the house.

Feet were pounding on the floor as if someone was leaping!

It was Aaron! Kerry could see him through the window. He was jumping and shouting!

"Charlie Greene, you cheat! You thought you could get away with it. You thought you were too clever to be caught, eh, Folsom? What do you say now? Ah, you don't say anything? How silent you are! You cannot speak any more. You're dead!"

Aaron laughed cruelly. "You didn't think I could do it, did you? Didn't think I had the guts, eh? Not until you saw the blade. And then, it was too late!"

Kerry and her grandfather watched as Aaron stood in the living room, leaping, lunging. The light in the house was dim, but they could see him thrusting the blade of the sword into the lampshade, then at a carved bronze pineapple, which clattered off the table.

"Take that, Greene! Take that, Folsom," he cried.

"Run home and call the police, Kerry," Grampy said. "Tell them our neighbor has lost it. I'll keep watching to make sure he doesn't leave."

Kerry refused to let go of her grandfather's hand. "Come on. You can't stay here! Oh, please come with me, Grampy!"

Kerry convinced her grandfather to join her, and the two hurried across the street. They rushed into the house. Kerry grabbed the phone. Her hands were shaking so much she could barely punch the number —9-1-1.

"There's a man across the street with a sword! He's acting crazy!" Kerry cried into the telephone.

"Kerry, here he comes. Tell the police to

hurry," Grampy said.

"He's walking onto our front yard!" Kerry continued. "Hurry!"

Aaron was out in front of the house now, sword in hand, hollering, "You called the police, Leo Poulson. I know you're in there. Your call to the police lead to the death of the finest man who ever lived. You killed a genius. Michael Cadden was a genius. He died in that flaming wreck, and he never did a bad thing in his life. Do you hear me, Leo Poulson? He was an innocent man. An innocent man pursued to his death by the police!"

Kerry thought she was going to faint as the blade cracked against the front door. The entire house seemed to tremble. Then Aaron walked across the front yard so that he stood in front of the window in the living room. He swung the blade against the glass and shattered the window. Kerry and her grandfather watched as Aaron made his way through the broken window into the house.

As Aaron came closer, the two ran into the kitchen and closed the heavy wooden door behind them. They huddled together and listened for the man's footsteps.

"I think he's coming," Kerry cried softly.

Without warning, the sword slammed into the wooden door that led to the kitchen.

"This is it, Grampy," Kerry cried. "We have nowhere left to hide."

"Ssh, Kerry. Keep real quiet. I think I hear something," her grandfather turned his head.

Suddenly the night filled with the wail of sirens.

"Oh, I hear it too! I can hear the sirens! The police are almost here!" Kerry rejoiced.

"Oh, thank God," her grandfather said.

The police swarmed the property and cornered Aaron Cadden. He put up no fight, but instead, broke down into tears. It took police only ten minutes to take him into custody.

"Everything is all right now, folks," a young police officer said. "Mr. Cadden won't be bothering you any more."

The police lead Cadden to the squad car as Kerry and her grandfather watched.

Kerry grabbed her grandfather's hand. "Grampy, are you okay?" she asked through tears.

"Yeah. I'm okay. What about you? Are you hurt?" Grampy asked. He hugged Kerry tightly.

"No. Just scared," Kerry replied.

"Well, he's gone now. This nightmare is finally over."

....

Two days later, Aaron Cadden was charged with double murder. Kerry's grandfather was down at the police station when he heard the news. He came home and told the family.

"But who did he kill?" Kerry asked.

"Greene and Folsom," her grandfather said. "He confessed to it. It seems that night 15 years ago, Aaron heard his father arguing with those two men. Apparently, Greene and Folsom were plotting to steal Michael's latest invention. According to Aaron, he burst into the room to help his father, but the two men laughed at him. So Aaron attacked them, using swordsmanship skills he learned for an acting role. Both Greene and Folsom were killed."

"But that's impossible," Kerry's dad

said. "Michael Cadden left a complete written confession. Michael admitted to killing the two men."

"Michael did that to spare his son. Michael took the blame for a crime he did not commit," Kerry's grandfather said. "After the divorce, Michael's ex-wife took Aaron to New York. Michael did not see Aaron for many years. Aaron eventually left New York and came back here to rebuild a relationship with his father. The two became quite close. After Aaron murdered those two men, Michael could not stand the thought of his son being taken away from him again. So, Michael took the blame, and wrote the fake confession." There was a look of sadness on Kerry's grandfather's face. "He died in that crash for his son."

"So where did Aaron go after he murdered those two guys? He didn't stay around here, did he?" Kerry asked.

"No. Aaron returned to New York, to his mother's apartment. But, the guilt he experienced from murdering two men tormented him. He broke down mentally and had to be committed to an expensive private hospital. Last summer, after Aaron Cadden's mother died, he moved back to the house his father once lived in. He planned to sell the place and get on with his life. But the old demons surfaced at the scene of his crimes, and he broke down mentally once again."

"Wow. What an ordeal you both went through. It scares me just to think about it," Kerry's dad said. "You two handling such a terrible situation alone!"

"Yeah, just imagine," Kerry's grandfather said, "a dumb kid and an even dumber old man, and we did just fine together."

Kerry giggled behind her hand.

Kerry's mom glanced at her father and her daughter. "I'm proud of you guys," she said, her voice thick with emotion. "I'm really proud."